Tales of The Haggis

The Saga of the
von Schnitzelgruber Clan
of Ochaye,
Isle of Dinafashyersel,
Scotland

by

Michael Davies

Tales of The Haggis

First Printing 2024

ISBN: 978-0-6459672-3-4

Published by The Mickie Dalton Foundation
NSW
Australia

To

Acknowledgements

Sincere thanks to those who supported this project:

Knickerflasher Twinkletits	Morale Officer
Hiram P Schnitzelgruber	Chief Haggis Trainer
Boobie McJugs	Political Officer
Shlomo Wong	Veterinary Consultant
Walter Hochenscheisenhaus	Wallaby Wrangler
Prudence Yamomoto	Sausage Decorator
Sarah Sparklemoose	ex-Governor of Alaska
Wolfgang Amadeus Mozart	Abattoir Manager
Mannie Ng	Firing Squad Leader
Daphne Snotgargler	Canteen Manager
Alphonse Khruschev	Communist Party Head
La Contessa di Alvaro di Pong	Termite Exterminator
Izzie Dead	Politician Taxidermist
Esmerelda Finklestein IV	Duck Sexer
Irene Pobblebonk	Frog
Tarquin de la Plonk, Seventh Earl of Piddlington, Keeper of the Queen's Ferrets and Right Royal Pain in the Arse	Garbage Truck Driver

Other Books by Michael Davies

The Nightmares of God
The Janus Conspiracy
A Friendly Killing
Helix Dreams
Helix – The Second Renaissance
Helix - Ascension
Accounts of a Killing
Dreamkill
Ready, Steady, KILL!
The Ninth of the Month Murders
The Death Gambit
The Internet Murders

For the Young Adults (12-18)
The Many Worlds of Mickie Dalton
The Many Galaxies of Mickie Dalton
The Many Universes of Mickie Dalton
The Strange World of Mark and Anna

For the 8-12 Age Group
The Quest for the Locket
The Julie Malloy Gang and the Smugglers
The Secret of Yuri Kirilenko
The United Nations and the Extra-Terrestrial
The Secret of Charlotte's Cello
The Star of the Yshan Kings
The War of the Yshan Empire
The Star of the New Yshan Empire
The Red Fog of Time
The Mysterious Recorder and The Door to Elsewhere
Prisoners of the Picture

For the Little Ones (3-5)
Mary's World

And in non-fiction
The Business School Approach to Writing Your Novel

Chapter 1 – The Clan von Schnitzelgruber

Australian history is full of well-worn anecdotes, ranging from ancient stories of the Dream Time through to modern tales of boring stuff like Captain Cook's landing, the founding of Parramatta and some bloke called John Kerr who nearly messed up the whole bloody thing.

Less is known about some episodes which, while not in the history books, had a massive impact on the social life and culture of Australia. One of these is the story of the ancient Clan von Schnitzelgruber from the small hamlet of Ochaye on the Isle of Dinafashyersel in northern Scotland.

Although the von Schnitzelgrubers had a long and glorious history in Scotland, our story begins in 1875 when the patriarch of the clan, Heinrich von Schnitzelgruber left Ochaye to move to Australia. Heinrich von Schnitzelgruber was a successful haggis-farmer when he travelled with his wife Zelda and they set up a small property in the Snowy Mountains. They had brought with them five pairs of breeding haggises.

They discussed the course of action thoroughly before leaving.

Chúng tôi đang di chuyển đến Úc
(We are moving to Australia)

Tại sao chúng tôi đang di chuyển đến Úc? Tôi không muốn đi Úc.
(Why are we moving to Australia? I don't want to go Australia.)

Tôi đã được cho biết là có một thị trường lớn cho sống haggises.
(I've been told that there's a huge market for live haggises.)

Những người mua haggises sống tại Úc?
(Who buys live haggises in Australia?)

Tất cả người Scotland quý tộc người Scotland khi William Wallace thực hiện tất cả những bộ phim lousy.
(All the Scottish nobles who left Scotland when William Wallace made all those lousy movies.)

Tại sao chúng tôi đang nói chuyện bằng tiếng Việt. Tôi nghĩ chúng ta là người Scotland.
(Why are we speaking in Vietnamese? I thought we were Scottish.)

Chúng tôi. Đây là Việt Nam? Tôi nghĩ rằng nó là Gaelic. Không có thắc mắc chúng ta có như vậy khó khăn trong siêu thị.
(We are. This is Vietnamese? I thought it was Gaelic. No wonder we have such difficulties in the Supermarket.)

(Nhưng liệu chúng ta có để mặc thể? Thể làm cho tôi arse nhìn chất béo.
But will we have to wear Lederhosen? Lederhosen make my arse look fat.)

Đó là áo.
(That's Austria.)

Sự khác biệt là gì?
(What's the difference?)

Khoảng 9.000 dặm.
(About 9,000 miles.)

Điều này thật điên rồ.
(This is crazy.)

Câm moo ngớ ngẩn và đi
và đóng gói. Và nguồn cấp
dữ liệu các haggises đầu
tiên.
*(Shut up you silly moo
and go and pack. And
feed the haggises first.)*

Five pairs of breeding haggises

Haggises thrived in the Snowy Mountains climate and the von Schnitzelgrubers found a ready market among the Scottish nobility who had long been deprived of the ancient Scottish sport of Haggis-hunting. The von Schnitzelgruber haggises were renowned for their speed and nimbleness which so improved in the Snowy diet that they soon became uncatchable to the footbound hunters, following the ancient Scottish tradition of being unable to ride a horse.

But the problem that soon arose was that the original Scottish haggises lived in the highlands and lived their lives on the steep slopes, following the sun from east to west and eating the fresh grass as it grew. Evolution had caused them to have longer right legs than left in order to move easily on the slopes. But in the southern hemisphere, the Coriolis Effect somehow made the haggises graze from west to east, and that meant they were unable to stand upright and always fell down the mountains. The newly bred haggises of the von Schnitzelgruber clan were successfully bred with left legs longer than the right and so thrived.

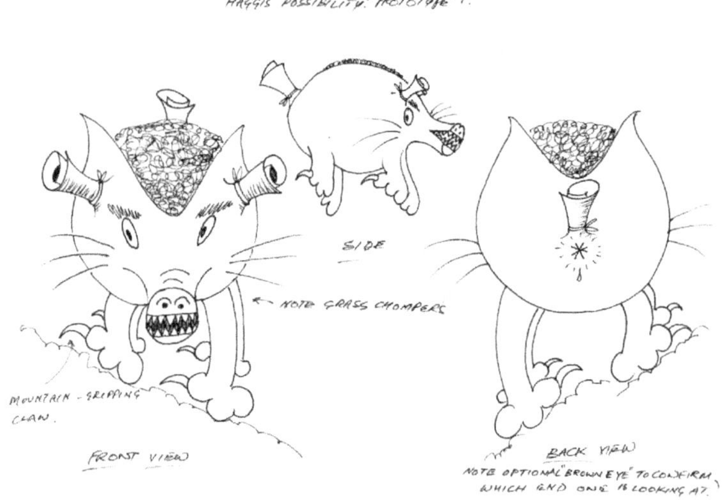

Heinrich and Zelda had two boys, Alphonse and Percy and they saw the market opportunity to breed haggis hounds that were skilled in hunting the haggises through any conditions. These were bred with right legs longer than the left and were trained to hunt from the opposite direction of the haggis grazing patterns and so made the haggises turn and run, immediately falling down the mountain where they could be collected by the Scottish man-servants.

However, as haggis breeding became more wide-spread with haggises being bred mainly as a food source, haggis

farms appeared in western NSW in the flat lands and within a few generations, the "Level Haggis" evolved with equi-length legs. This resulted in time in the national sport of haggis hound trials being developed. (See further on).

Evolution of the Tree-Climbing Haggis

After two seasons of heavy flooding in western NSW, many of the equi-legged haggises took to climbing trees and breeding in nests they constructed. This resulted in the phenomenon of "Drop-Haggises" as young haggises jumped on passing people, inflicting serious scratches and other injuries.

A program of culling the tree-climbing version was successful and this danger passed. However, some locals in their enthusiasm for destroying the tree-climbing haggises, rather overdid the process and caused some distress among both residents and local fauna alike.

Evolution of the Sea-Going Haggis

Many roaming flocks of escaped haggises that left the breeding farms after the floods reached the south-eastern coast of Victoria. They swam across the Tasman and invaded New Zealand, becoming a major problem, competing with the sheep for grass and causing serious damage to the tourist trade.

Even worse, many of them became carnivorous and began to attack the sheep, tending to concentrate on the soft underbelly, causing a large population of hollowed out sheep.

With no natural predator, they quickly became a plague until, hearing of this, the Reverend Hieronymus von Schnitzelgruber sailed over to NZ to investigate the problem.

He spent six weeks of prayer and fasting in the Southlands, breaking the ritual only to eat several pounds of smoked fish and drink lots of beer in the local pubs, he finally approached the Town Council of a small community at the base of Mount Cook and during a town hall meeting, rose to speak.

"What have you to say to us?" asked the Mayor. "And will you introduce yourself?"

"I am the Reverend Hieronymus von Schnitzelgruber," said the priest. "And I can remove this plague of invading haggises."

A murmur of mixed wonder and anger ran through the audience, because while they had heard of the exploits of the von Schnitzelgruber clan in breeding the finest haggises and haggis hounds, they were also aware that their current dreadful crisis could be laid at the feet of this family.

The council members looked at each other with some doubt but also hope.

"And just how will you do this?" the Mayor asked.

"I will perform..." Hieronymus von Schnitzelgruber stood straight as a ray of sunshine shone through the window and onto his face. The audience went deathly silent. "I will perform... The Rite of Exorcism of the Haggis," he proclaimed.

A gasp of mixed fear and wonder ran through the hall, together with whispers of, *"The Exorcism of the Haggis! That has not been seen for centuries! What manner of man is this?"*

When the disturbance settled, the Mayor rose to his feet.

"Then by the power invested in me as Mayor of this Town and owner of the local fish and chip shop,[1] I command you, Reverend Hieronymus von Schnitzelgruber to rid our land of the this dreadful pestilence."

---

[1] *(pronounced: 'fush 'n chup shup')*

The Reverend bowed and walked out through the silent audience to have lunch of smoked cod and beer in the *"Sheep and Kiwi Arms"* pub next door.

The following morning, a cold, clear day of bright sunshine and light breezes, the townspeople gathered at the foot of Mount Cook. Before any of them arrived, the Reverend Hieronymus von Schnitzelgruber had already taken his place, sitting on a blanket in deep prayer, clasping his bagpipes.

After the crowd had gone silent, the priest rose to his feet and faced the mountain. With one, sweeping motion, he removed his kilt.

A whisper ran through the crowd.

"He wears the von Schnitzelgruber tartan underpants," they murmured in awe. "No such sight has been seen here for many years."

"And the String Vest of Authority!" murmured another. "With a white wing collar and black bow tie! These are the trappings of great power!"

"The Exorcism begins!" exclaimed another, a tremble of fear in her voice.

The Reverend picked up his bagpipes and began pumping the bag while hideous noises emanated from the innards, but after much thumping, a pure, clear note sounded and echoed onto the Mount Cook slopes before giving way to a wondrous melody.

"He plays the Johann Sebastian Bach Toccata and Fugue in D Minor!" whispered the mayor. "What sort of God-like powers does this man hold?"

The Reverend began marching up the slopes of the Mountain, but two hundred metres up, he made a ninety degree turn to the left and marched further.

"He turns Widdershins!" exclaimed the town's treasurer. "What can withstand the power of this exorcism?"

The priest turned right again and began ascending the slopes, soon vanishing among the hills, though the sounds of the pipes and the Great D Minor Toccata and Fugue continued to be heard.

All day, the crowd stayed to witness this earth-shaking event and while the priest appeared only on rare occasions, the sound of the music never stopped.

At five o'clock, the crowd stirred as the sound of the music climbed in volume and the Reverend Hieronymus von Schnitzelgruber appeared, walking down the hill toward them. Finally, he stopped playing, donned his kilt again and bowed to the Mayor.

"Same time tomorrow, then?" he said. "Now, where's that pub? All this exorcism stuff has given me a hell of a thirst. I'm as dry as a dead dingo's donger, mate."

The next morning the procedure was repeated and again on the third day.

As he returned to the watching crowd on that last day, the reverend approached the mayor.

"You'll notice," he said, "there's not a trace of a haggis anywhere around. Give it a couple more days and there won't be a single haggis anywhere in the country."

Almost weeping, the Mayor clutched the priest's hands.

"How can a grateful nation possibly repay you?" he sobbed.

"No fee," replied the Reverend Hieronymus von Schnitzelgruber. "This was the least I could do, given that my family was to blame for this horror."

With that, he left, never to be seen again in the Land of The Long White Cloud.

True to his word, within days of performing this rite, all traces of the NZ haggis had disappeared. To this day, New Zealand sheep-farmers celebrate Haggis-Banning Day, or in Kiwi, "Huggus-Bunning Day" with a re-enactment of the Saint Hieronymus rites on Mount Cook. Being selected to play the role of Saint Hieronymus is considered a huge honour and young men compete over a six-week selection trial period. Naturally, an essential qualification is having great legs and being to play the bagpipes in your underpants while freezing your balls off on Mount Cook.

Evolution of National Haggis-Hound Trials

Haggis Hound trials became a national event in the 1930s and 1940s. The object was to separate the Queen Haggis out from the rest of the haggis flock and drive her into a marked enclosure on the far side of the field. Initially, standard Haggis-Hounds were used and the entire event was conducted at ground level. Huge crowds came to watch these trials and newsreel films of the events were highly popular in cinemas around the land.

But haggises were intelligent creatures and developed the art of protection of the Queen Haggis by circling round her, thus requiring the Gliding Hound to be developed. Alphonse became famous for his training techniques in which the specially-bred Gliding Hound grew a sizeable membrane between the legs on each side and by extending them could glide significant distances, often as much as thirty metres. Haggis hound trials thus became a test of the hound's ability to leap from outside the pack of haggises and glide a complex path to the Queen Haggis, separating her out from the guarding Soldier Haggises and drive her into the fenced enclosure.

Aficionados of the sport claimed that the *"glisser à droit"* demonstrated the true technique, while the *"glisser à gauche"* was by far the least skilful and less attractive approach and invariably scored worse with the judges.

However, the sport was badly damaged by the great Fart Propulsion Scandal of 1969. At the Haggis Hound Grand Finals in Windsor, the massive spectator crowd was astounded when the lead hound belonging to Perseus von Schnitzlegruber, a minor breeder of hounds and a distant relative of the main line of the von Schnitzelgruber Clan was seen to soar several hundred feet into the air before arrowing down almost vertically onto the Queen Haggis surrounded by her protective guard of soldier haggises.

The collision caused the instant death of both Queen and hound, leaving a massive pile of guts, bone and blood on the grass. Competition referees were called immediately and delicately poked their way through the ugly mess. After a few minutes, one of them called out a discovery of something unusual, a small, metallic object, roughly spherical in shape but with a large hole on one side and a nozzle opposite the hole, and two straps.

Later forensic examination assisted by aeronautical engineers decided that the device was strapped over the anus of the haggis hound with the hole over the anal exit and the nozzle pointing backwards. A fart from the hound caused an automatic compression of the thick air and a spark ignited the compressed gas which then blew out the nozzle providing a significant fart-assisted jet stream. Further post mortem examination of the hound revealed that it had been fed a meal of Coco-Pops just before the event and this had generated major flatulence leading to several fart-assisted reheat jet pulses that had lifted the hound to an altitude of well over two hundred metres.

A tribunal of the Stewards of the Haggis Hound Trials Association held that Perseus von Schnitzlegruber was guilty of unlawfully applying engineering assistance to his hounds. He was banned for life from the sport and stripped of the trophy he had won in 1965.

The Children of Heinrich von Schnitzelgruber

Percy von Schnitzelgruber

Percy von Schnitzelgruber went into Kangaroo training to solve the problems of transport across the Nullarbor. He was the primary designer of the Nullarbor Stage Coach and trained the Big Red Fliers to leap in pairs and in succession in rubberised harnesses to eliminate whip-lash for the passengers.

An unexpected side effect of this technology was that the vibrations of the harness caused a curious soporific effect, not just on the passengers but on wildlife along the way. As a result, the passing of the stagecoach left sleeping kangaroos, emus and other small fauna by the tracks and some were collected by locals as an easily caught addition to the larder. To avoid the effect on the driver and crew, they had to wear metal helmets with rubberised linings and ear plugs. But the stage coach company exploited this effect by advertising the trips as "sleeper coaches."

Ned von Schnitzelgruber

Percy's son was Ned von Schnitzelgruber who became an outlaw, robbing the Nullarbor Coaches pulled by the kangaroos trained by his elder brother. Notorious for wearing a coal scuttle on his head, he was known as "Wrong Way Schnitzelgruber" for his propensity for racing off after a robbery, going the wrong way and right into the patrolling local police. He only escaped because the cops tended to shit their drawers with laughter at the sight, allowing him to run away from them.

He was eventually apprehended by a particularly humourless cop, Senior Sergeant Audrey Li Wong, a Bolivian immigrant outside the small town of Roo Dropping, New South Wales. He was sentenced to spend five years listening to speeches in the State Upper House and although he survived this brutal punishment, he lived for the next five years in an insane asylum, muttering, "He's gone troppo, Mr Speaker," and similar incomprehensible phrases.

This history of criminal behaviour and utter incompetence made him an ideal figure in New South Wales politics and he was later recruited by one of the major parties and later served as Treasurer in the NSW State parliament.

Eurydice von Schnitzelgruber

Eurydice von Schnitzelgruber was the daughter of Alphonse and also the undisputed Clan beauty. But in addition, she was renowned as a poet of national and international fame.

These are some samples of her works.

Meditations on a Hunkenscheisenhauser

"My Love is like a royal blue Hunkenscheisenhauser.
It glows like perriwinkels in a stream of porridge.
Whoflungdung and whatchermercallit.
Carry on, Admiral."

Reflections on an Aromatic Marsupial

"Oh Pooh!
It stinks!
Who pooped here?
Why, a Koala Bear!
A very ancient Koala Bear.
Little Bastard.
Carry on, General."

Ariadne's Protest

"Don't Come The Raw Prawn with me,
Mate.
My dad's a General.
Wallabies live in my bedroom
And cane toads
So bloody watch it.
Carry on, Colonel."

Ode to Tucker

"Abalone, prawns and scallops
Aussie seafood tucker
Drink till we're legless
And rat-arsed.
Carry on, Corporal."

Critics were delighted with *"Ode to Tucker"* when it was first published in the *"Sydney Morning Herald Literary Supplement."* Poetry Critic, Erik Streetcrawler said, "Ms von Schnitzelgruber has so eloquently caught the spirit of the Australian cultural ethos with this passionate ode to our cuisine. She is rapidly becoming an icon in Australian literature and a national treasure."

Eurydice's next work produced an even stronger reaction.

Revelations on The Homeland

"Pommies are rubbish.
Can't play cricket.
Never wash.
Can't surf.
Useless gits.
Carry on, Major."

This last work was considered by most critics to be her most magnificent. Literary writer in *"The Australian,"* Booby McJugs wrote that, "This wonderful verse evokes the finest qualities of Australian pride and a maturity that has far surpassed the old sense of colonialism that has haunted so many Australian writers."

A national poll was taken in Australia as to whether this verse should replace the National Anthem but was very narrowly defeated by just a few percentage points.

In 1966, Eurydice von Schnitzelgruber entered the Miss Australia beauty pageant as the first stage of fulfilling her dream of becoming Miss World. However, during the preliminary regional stages, she was ejected from the competition for bashing Miss Roo Dropping, Diane Piddlington-Smythe on the head, screaming "Who ever heard of an Australian called Piddlington-Smythe?" and then insisting on reading her poems on stage.

As she left the hall, escorted by several security men, she was heard to yell out to the judge, Colonel Wong Yong Lee, "That's the last blowjob you get from me, you miserable little German turd!"

To many feminists, this cry reflected the tone of defiance and anger common in Beauty Pageants, up there in power and historical significance with tales of the Eureka Stockade and was adopted as the unofficial motto of entrants.

Sales of her collected works shot up and she retired on the proceeds to her farm in Widdle-Widdle, New South Wales to grow lantana bushes for commercial sale.

Wotan von Schnitzelgruber

Wotan von Schnitzelgruber, a late addition to Alphonse's offspring, enlisted in the Australian Army to fight in WWI after changing his name to Hochscheisenhaus to avoid sounding like a German. His brigade was sent to France and he fought in the little-known battle of la Petite Eglise du Lac des Deux Montagnes d'Avignon where, with 25 other troops on patrol they encountered a similar

German patrol in dense fog. Both sides turned and ran and both fell into their trenches, suffering several broken legs and bruises. Rescued by a later patrol of his own brigade, he was patched up and transferred to the 45th Woolloomooloo Scouts Troop where he served for three years before he was arrested for inappropriate training methods which largely consisted of having the boys strip naked and perform erotic dances. After five years in Long Bay Gaol, he was released but never heard of again, though some rumours placed him as a Bishop in a remote Catholic diocese in the Northern Territories.

Lochinvar von Schnitzelgruber

Lochinvar von Schnitzelgruber, the son of Eurydice and her partner, Albert Higginbottom, became famous as the renowned choreographer for the nationally-acclaimed Roo Dropping Symphony Orchestra and Haggis Ballet Company. His particular talent for developing intricate dance routines for haggises reached its peak when he developed the extraordinary ballet, *"Haggis Pond"* for the Symphony Orchestra and Ballet Company.

All went well during the weeks of rehearsals, but when the first dress rehearsal was held, the haggises went berserk and attacked each other in a savage bloodbath.

The scene was horrendous. Bits of haggis were strewn all over the stage, together with scraps of tutu and spouts of blood sprayed down into the orchestra stall, causing horror among the members of the symphony orchestra. Most resigned, never to return, leaving only enough members to form the Roo Dropping String Quartet as the surviving musical talent in the town.

Animal psychologists have theorised that the white tutus triggered an ancestral memory of an ancient Scottish predator and caused widespread panic. Some of the haggises escaped and fled to the surrounding countryside. There are still tales of wild haggises in tatty tutus roaming the hills around Roo Dropping and attacking hikers and while the local council has declared such rumours to be mere fable, nobody will venture beyond the town limits after dark.

Lochinvar von Schnitzelgruber left the town a day later and has never been seen again. The *"Haggis Pond"* ballet has never been performed in public.

Galahad von Schnitzelgruber

Galahad von Schnitzelgruber was always a problem to the family. His schooldays were marked by a constant inability to learn anything at all and he showed no interest in any of the family businesses. He joined the army at the age of eighteen and finally found something that interested him when he was introduced to guns at the shooting range. He became fairly adept at gun maintenance and eventually left the army to set up his own gun manufacturing business. However, none of his designs proved effective and his business was nearly on its last legs when he designed and produced the prototype of the reverse shooter handgun, which he believed would be popular for its ability to shoot behind the holder and thus create total surprise for any potential criminal attempting an assault from the rear.

After several years of engineering attempts, the first of the new handguns was taken to the range for a public demonstration. Tragically, Galahad died at the first attempt to fire the weapon when the bullet entered his chest. For some reason, the design was not successful and the business was closed down. An analysis by weapons experts concluded that Galahad had made one major miscalculation in his design by failing to realise that when shooting the pistol at an enemy behind him, the shooter's own body remained in place between gun and attacker.

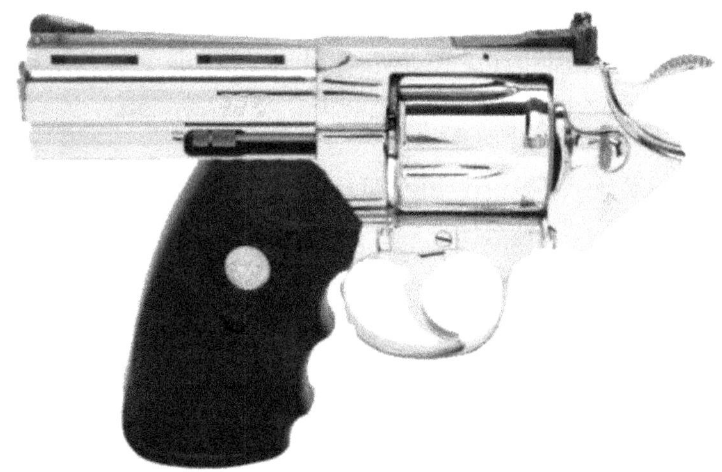

Brünnhilde von Schnitzelgruber

Brünnhilde von Schnitzelgruber followed the path of her great-aunt, Eurydice von Schnitzelgruber of becoming a writer when her first romantic novel, *"Rhonda Finds Happiness in Rome"* was published in 1975. It sold well and her second romantic novel, *"Matilda Finds Happiness in Munich"* was produced later in 1976. It was followed by *"Deborah Finds Happiness in Dorking"* and soon after, by *"Lavinia Finds Happiness in Liverpool"* and by this time, Brünnhilde von Schnitzelgruber was the highest-earning writer in Australia. By the time *"Zelda Finds Happiness in Zurich"* was published in 1985, more than twenty of her books had been released and all had shot to Number One on the best seller lists, particularly the New York Times Literary Supplement.

At that time, Leviticus Brown, a lecturer in literature at the University of Roo Dropping in New South Wales wrote a critical article on the works of Brünnhilde von Schnitzelgruber.

"After checking through each of the books of Brünnhilde von Schnitzelgruber," he wrote, "it is glaringly obvious that all her books are identical, and that each new work was produced after using the "Global Replace" function in the word processing software to change the names of the two main protagonists and places, but that was all. Beyond that, every book is word for word the same as every other book."

Mr Brown went on to comment, "This says nothing good about the ethics of the author, the ethics and literary skills of the publishers and the intelligence and analytical talents of the women who read this garbage."

A senior editor for the publishing industry and spokeswoman for the Australian Guild of Women Writers, Ms Knickerflasher Twinkletits was harshly critical of the article.

"If the story is brilliant, imaginative, creative and touches the soul of its women readers, then the tale can be repeated again and again and will always have the same result. Our readers don't care about repeated themes, they buy the books of Brünnhilde von Schnitzelgruber in order to experience the moving emotional sensations that she produces and learn about the exotic locations in which she places her stories. Anyway, all romance novels have the same theme. Only a man could write this criticism, because it's only men who want stories to be different and original, but everybody in the publishing industry knows that all men are beer-swilling, sports-obsessed, illiterate oafs who don't read books, which is why we don't bother producing books for the bastards."

At time of writing, Brünnhilde's fortieth book, *"Hortense Finds Happiness in Hawaii"* was hitting the stands with advance sales already breaking all records. She is believed to be working on another book, *"Gabrielle Finds Happiness in Gundawindi."*

After two years of intense lobbying by the Australian Guild of Women Writers, Professor Leviticus Brown was fired from his post at the University of Roo Dropping after a committee of women professors found him guilty of anti-feminist philosophies. However, he proceeded to make an absolute fortune writing a series of erotic bondage novels under the name of Fifi La Boom Boom, beginning with *"Oxana's Travails in Oxford,"* which won the International Prize for Steamy Bondage in 2001, followed soon after by *"Belinda's Travails in Brisbane," "Shania's Travails in Shanghai"* and his most recent work, *"Grizelda's Travails in Grimsby,"* which has already topped the Australian best-seller lists and has had similar results throughout Europe where it has been translated into fourteen languages.

Mr Brown's publisher has indicated that his client is working on a new book, believed to be entitled, *"Magdalena's Travails in Moscow."* A first printing is expected to be in the one million plus copies.

To date, he has refused to join the Australian Guild of Women Writers despite frequent invitations. However, prior to publication of this book, Leviticus Brown was reported to have told his brother that he was planning on joining the Guild under his pen name and then using his connections to be invited to appear on the television program, *"The World of Romance Novels"* on which he would, as he put it, "Reveal to the silly bitches that these best-selling novels were all written by a bloke and they're all exactly the same except for the names of the bloke and the shielah and the town where they get their kit off and have at it like rampant rabbits. It will make their bloody heads explode."

Agamemnon von Schnitzelgruber

Agamemnon von Schnitzelgruber had dreamed of being a pilot since early childhood. He was eighteen when the Second World War broke out in Europe and he immediately set sail for England and enlisted in the Royal Air Force. Having no formal education, he was initially enlisted as an Aircraftsman Second Class (known colloquially as an AC Plonk) and assigned to Kitchen Porter duties. However, through sheer determination and persistence, he was at last able to get an application for flying training accepted by the RAF as pilot losses were increasing.

However, his first training flight in a Tiger Moth indicated that his pilot aptitude skills were impressive for their complete absence. His flight instructor, Flying Officer Adrian "Steely-Eyed Acc" Hedgetrimmer reported to the Squadron Commander, "I have never seen such a cack-handed, display of utter fuckwitted incompetence in my life and that includes the time we experimented with teaching chimpanzees to fly in the simulators. He can't tell a rudder from the landing gear and he couldn't grasp the idea that he was supposed to hold onto the control column. This bloke should never be allowed within a bloody mile of an airfield, never mind an actual plane. Maybe we should hand him over to the Krauts and they'll take him as a pilot."

The idea struck a chord with the Squadron Commander, Squadron Leader Reginald "Tottie-Hunter" Smythe-Smythe (pronounced Wellington) who passed it up to the Wing who passed it up to Group who passed it up to Adastral House who passed it to Fighter Command where one of the most successful wartime plans was developed.

Six weeks later, Flight-Sergeant Agamemnon von Schnitzelgruber was taken to a secret airfield on the South Coast where he was briefed by Flight Lieutenant Randolph ("Randy") "Tit Groper" Haynes.

""You're an absolute natural, laddie," said Titgroper Haynes. "Your flight instructor at Hornchurch, Flying Officer Hedgetrimmer said he had never seen such astonishing pilot aptitude as yours."

"That's fabulous," said Flight-Sergeant Agamemnon von Schnitzelgruber. "Does that mean I'll become a Spitfire Pilot?"

"Damn right!" said Titgroper Haynes. "In fact, you were so astonishing that we've decided to bypass the training and assign you to a fighter squadron immediately."

"Wow," said Agamemnon. "My family will be amazed."

"They surely will. So here's what we're going to do. As you know, we've lost a lot of pilots in recent weeks and there's a bit of a push on for a big operation in a couple of days. So we're just going to show you how to start up the engine of a Spitfire and you'll be just fine after that. In fact, you'll be taken to your new squadron tonight."

That afternoon, Flight-Sergeant Agamemnon von Schnitzelgruber was taken to a captured Messerschmitt Me-

109 which had been repainted in RAF colours and shown how to get the engine started. Having no knowledge of aircraft types, von Schnitzelgruber did not spot the difference in makes.

Later that night, he was dressed in the uniform taken from a captured Luftwaffe pilot shot down the previous week, briefed further on his mission to claim that he was a pilot but suffering from mild memory loss, filled up with cheap scotch and then flown out by night in a Lysander aircraft and put down in a field near a Luftwaffe fighter station where he fell asleep.

He was found soon after dawn, just before the RAF launched a major attack on the town nearby as part of the plan. In panic, the Luftwaffe police who had found him, raced him straight to a waiting Me-29 and strapped him in. Still suffering a massive hangover, Flight-Sergeant Agamemnon von Schnitzelgruber started up the engine, released the brakes and began taxying out with the other fighters. Over the next fifteen minutes, he managed to run into eight of the fighters on his way out to the start of the runway and when he opened up the throttle, he ploughed into a whole line of fighters waiting to get started. Fires ignited in most of them and these exploded, taking out the rest of the squadron and although a few Me-29s were able to get airborne, a flight of Hurricanes waiting nearby and briefed on what would happen were able to shoot down all of them.

In the exhilaration of flight, Flight-Sergeant Agamemnon von Schnitzelgruber opened up the throttle and managed to get airborne but was then shot to pieces like the others by a Hurricane piloted by an Australian pilot,

Sergeant Bluey Murray who received a Distinguished Flying Medal some weeks later.

Flight-Sergeant Agamemnon von Schnitzelgruber was buried with full military honours by the Luftwaffe who believed he was the pilot who was actually held captive in England.

The RAF awarded him the Distinguished Service Medal (Posthumous) as the only pilot who had ever destroyed almost an entire squadron of enemy fighters singlehandedly.

Aphrodite von Schnitzelgruber

Aphrodite von Schnitzelgruber was always destined for high political office. At the age of six, she was expelled from her primary school after being found to have been running a protection racket in the school. Together with two assistants, she would demand another child's lunch money once a week and share it with her assistants, 70% for herself, the rest split between the others who were only on occasions required to administer a severe spanking on the behind to the resister.

Transferred to another primary school under threat of prosecution, her new racket was to keep her own lunch money and demand either the first course or the dessert course of the school lunches from a series of victims each day. This lasted a year before being found to be stealing tins of custard from the school canteen and selling them to the local grocery store. Rather than continue to high school, she embarked on a life of crime similar to that of her great-uncle, Ned von Schnitzelgruber, attacking children on their way to school and stealing any valuables they had.

In her later teens, a most rewarding path was found when she began stealing live haggises from the breeding farms around her town of Roo Dropping and selling them to a private vendor of haggises who supplied a number of grocery chains around NSW. This made her a wealthy woman in her mid-twenties, but she was arrested when one of the grocery stores, angered by the fact that she had sold them a branded haggis with the brand still in place, reported her to the state police. After a short trial, she served two years in the women's penitentiary at Silverwater.

Upon her release, she was approached by several political parties in the state who offered her a safe seat with a consensus that with her background and experience she would make an excellent State Treasurer, as had her great-uncle Ned, but she declined and formed her own party, the Haggis Party with a policy of breeding haggises for release into the wild for hunters, exactly as had been the original policy of Heinrich von Schnitzelgruber when he first came to Australia. She was able to win election in her home town of Roo Dropping and became the unofficial advisor to the Minister for Finance for the government of the day for several years before her tragic death when attacked by a pack of angry haggises in the wilderness near the town.

The Last of the von Schnitzelgruber Clan

By 1982, only one Schnitzelgruber family remained, the previous generation having produced only one offspring, Dmitri. Little is known of him, as he produced no school work that was recorded, failed all his school leaving exams and there is no record of his ever having worked for a salary with any organisations.

However, in 1990, his application for a passport was received by the Australian government and one was issued. His place of birth was shown as Wagga Wagga, the home of the original haggis breeding farm and his occupation shown as "Haggis Groomer."

Travel records show him as flying to the United States of America and later marrying a distant relative of Donald Trump, a later president.

No record of any marriage exists and nothing more is known of Dmitri von Schnitzelgruber.